PERPETRATOR PRANKS

PATTI BENNING

SUMMER PRESCOTT BOOKS PUBLISHING

Copyright 2025 Summer Prescott Books

All Rights Reserved. No part of this publication nor any of the information herein may be quoted from, nor reproduced, in any form, including but not limited to: printing, scanning, photocopying, or any other printed, digital, or audio formats, without prior express written consent of the copyright holder.

**This book is a work of fiction. Any similarities to persons, living or dead, places of business, or situations past or present, is completely unintentional.

CHAPTER ONE

"She's not going to make it."

"Yes, she is." Penelope Montgomery clutched the windowsill, her breath fogging the glass as she stared out at the parking lot, her jaw clenched and her eyes blazing as if sheer determination could prevent a disaster.

"Ten bucks says she's going to hit that gray car." Cody Brooks, the motel's only employee, appeared unconcerned. His arms were crossed, and he was leaning his hip against the solid wood of the front desk, his head tilted slightly to one side as he watched the scene that was unfolding outside.

"Don't gamble at work," Penny muttered, not taking her eyes from the window.

Sadie Barton, who had walked in on the worrying

scene from her latest expedition to the laundry room, joined her best friend and their young employee at the window, where she craned her neck over Penny's shoulder to see an ancient, boxy, sedan that was the size of a boat and seemed to have the turning radius to match, laboriously backing out of a parking spot. After backing up two feet, the driver straightened their wheels incrementally, then pulled forward until the front grille of the vehicle was nearly touching the back bumper of Sadie's SUV, then backed up another few feet before repeating the process.

"She shouldn't be driving," Sadie murmured. "How long has this been going on?"

"It's been about two minutes since she first started her car," Penny replied.

She winced as the old vehicle came dangerously close to backing into the gray car Cody had pointed out was in the danger zone. Cody looked smug at the near miss, and Penny shot him a dirty look.

"You're not the one who pays our liability insurance," she muttered. "Our premiums are going to go up if she hits a guest's vehicle, and if *that* happens, it's going to be that much longer until we can give you a raise. So, if I were you, I'd wipe that smile off your face."

His expression sobered immediately, only to brighten a second later. "Wait, I'm getting a raise?"

Penny gave a long suffering sigh. Sadie had known her long enough to understand that she was mostly just teasing, but Cody had been working for them for less than a month. It was his first job, and she knew he was still nervous about messing up and getting fired. Penny probably wasn't helping.

"You're getting a raise as soon as we can afford it," Sadie told him. "We don't *want* to pay our employees minimum wage. Don't hold us to this, but we're hoping we'll be able to offer you at least a small raise by the end of summer."

It was May, so the end of summer was still a long way off, but Cody looked thrilled at the prospect. Sadie understood. The minimum wage in Georgia wasn't exactly much to make a living on. She wished they could afford to pay him more, but it just wasn't in the cards right now. She and Penny owned Sit, Stay, Sleep Motel and Boarding, and even they only drew enough of a salary to survive off of. Since they both lived at the motel, housing expenses were something neither of them needed to worry about… for now. She knew Penny was getting tired of living in a motel room, but they were still at the stage where they needed to pour most of their profits back into their business.

And it was paying off. The motel was doing better than they had dared hope when they first opened it last summer, but there was still a long list of repairs and upgrades they wanted to make. Sadie wanted more kennels for the dogs and an indoor area she could use for lessons and activities. Penny wanted to continue upgrading the motel rooms and, at some point, wanted to plan an addition for the motel side of the business as well. *That* was a long way off, but it didn't feel like an impossible dream anymore.

"There she goes." Penny gave a sigh of relief. "See? I told you she wouldn't hit anything."

"I bet she will next time," Cody said. "She almost hit *me* the last time she was here. That woman's going to kill someone if she doesn't stop driving."

"I'm siding with Cody on this one," Sadie said. "Loretta's a liability on the road… not just to the cars in our parking lot, but to every other person who's on the road with her."

"She must be a better driver than we think, because she's still driving, and that car doesn't have a dent on it," Penny said.

That was true. The old sedan had sun-faded paint

and rust-eaten side panels, but there was no sign that the vehicle had ever been damaged in a collision.

"It looks like she hasn't even driven it in a decade," Sadie muttered. "I bet you anything she only took it out again so she could harass us."

"You're just grumpy because you don't like her," Penny said.

She turned away from the window and jiggled her mouse to wake up her laptop's screen. Cody resumed cleaning the glass now that the excitement was over, and Sadie glanced at her watch. She should get back to work soon, but there was nothing urgent that needed her attention this very second. That meant she had time to bicker with Penny, one of her favorite pastimes.

"I still can't believe that you don't dislike her," Sadie said. "You *know* she's behind all those bad reviews we've been getting, and I'm pretty sure last time she was here, she stole that box of tissues we keep in the lobby. *And* she stole my spring garden gnome."

Penny gave her an unreadable look. "Sure, *she's* the one who stole your gnome. I don't even know where you keep finding those things. They're so creepy."

"They're not creepy," Sadie said. "They're cute."

Penny gave an exaggerated shudder, and out of the corner of his mouth Cody muttered, "They are kind of creepy, actually."

"Fine, gnomes aside… we really should just ban her, Penny."

"I feel bad for her, all right?" her friend said. "She's got to be almost ninety, and she lives all alone in that big house. It's not like her bed-and-breakfast is going to become competition for us any time soon. I don't think she's been able to keep the place up on her own for years. This 'feud' with us that she's made up seems to have given her a new lease on life. I don't want to take that away from her. Besides, we were able to get those reviews taken down since they were clearly a targeted attack so we aren't any worse off for it."

"I just hope Tanisha didn't see any of them," Sadie said. "We haven't gotten any cancellation emails, have we?"

Penny double-clicked to open the email app. "Nope, there's some spam mail, but that's it. I don't think she's going to cancel. She seemed pretty excited about this."

Tanisha Verdan was a travel vlogger who had arranged to stay for a week at the motel to film for her vlog. Not only was she going to feature the motel on her vlog, she was also paying for two rooms at full price all week – one for her, and one for her videographer. Sadie had no idea why she would choose their motel, of all places, but she wasn't about to look a gift horse in the mouth. This could be huge for them, and she was determined to make sure everything went perfectly.

She was a little worried that Murphy's Law was going to crop up when they least expected it, because that was the sort of luck they seemed to have. She wasn't normally a superstitious person, but Tanisha had specifically asked to stay in Room Ten, which was where a string of murders had occurred a few years ago, and that seemed like a bad omen to start things out on.

She and Penny had been going overboard with cleaning all week, which was why Cody was cleaning the windows even though they really didn't need it. He carefully moved the Wi-Fi router from the one spot on the windowsill where it seemed to get a decent signal so he could clean behind it, and her eyes fixed on the mess of cords that trailed off of it.

It wasn't something she'd never noticed before, but now she realized just how bad it looked. Her eyes went up to the overhead lights. Was one of them flickering? And the tile floor… they'd cleaned and scrubbed it to within an inch of its life, but the grout was still stained in some places. The chairs against the far wall were all uncomfortable plastic monstrosities. Should they have bought new ones over the weekend?

"We should check the rooms again," Penny said, giving voice to Sadie's sudden panic that all of their work hadn't been good enough. "Oh, and one of us needs to talk to the guest in Room Two."

Sadie forced her thoughts away from the vlogger's upcoming visit and wracked her mind trying to remember who was staying in Room Two.

"That's that woman, right? The one who asked whether we had weekly rates?"

"Yeah, her," Penny said, "She paid up through Wednesday night, and she said she was going to stop in yesterday to pay for the next couple of days, but she never did. I'm not sure if she's planning on staying longer or not, but I don't want her to leave without paying for last night."

"She *is* still here, right?" Sadie asked, glancing through the window, out at the parking lot. She didn't know which vehicle belonged to the Room Two guest, but Penny, who handled most of the motel side of the business, did.

She nodded and said, "She drives that burgundy

minivan. What should I tell her about the weekly rates? I know we've discussed it in the past, but we haven't settled on anything."

"Shoot, I don't know," Sadie said. "Let's take a look at what other motels in the area offer and try to be somewhere in their ballpark. We should figure out how long we can let someone stay before they get tenant's rights, too. We don't want to be stuck trying to evict someone who won't leave."

Her friend nodded and glanced out the window again, where she saw something that made her expression brighten. "Oh, that's so sweet!"

"What?" Sadie tried to peer out the window, but Penny put an arm out to hold her back. Cody, however, got a view of whatever Penny was looking at, and wrinkled his nose.

"Ugh, mushy stuff. I'm going to start emptying the garbage cans if you're done needing me to do stuff in here."

"Start in the laundry room, and empty the lint traps while you're at it," Penny said.

Cody grabbed his cleaning supplies and vanished through the door into the laundry room just as the lobby door opened and Sam Walker, Sadie's handsome boyfriend, who also happened to be their long-term tenant and landscaping expert, walked in. He held a bouquet of spring wildflowers in one hand, which he held out to Sadie, who took them with a grin.

"These are lovely, Sam, thank you," she said after she held the bouquet to her nose and inhaled deeply. "I have a vase upstairs. I can put them right here on the front desk. This will really brighten the lobby."

I should get you flowers more often, Sam signed to her. *I saw them while I was walking Briar and Rose. The flower garden by the old shed still blooms in the springtime, even without care.*

"Maybe we can start tending to it again," Sadie said. "We should try to get those paths cleaned up this year, anyway."

Even though Sam didn't work for them, in fact, ever since he started dating Sadie, he had refused to allow them to pay him a cent for anything he did on the motel's grounds, it had become natural to include him in their plans. He lived right next to the motel, in a small yellow house that he had a multi-year lease agreement on. Even though he had signed the lease with the previous owner, legally, they had to honor it. Sadie wouldn't even dream of renting the house to someone else by this point. She loved having Sam so close by.

"Oh shoot," Penny hissed.

She reached out to pull the blinds across the lobby window, then hurried around the front desk to turn the deadbolt on the door. Finally, she reached over and turned the lobby lights off, leaving the three of them standing in silence in the dim room.

CHAPTER TWO

"What is it?" Sadie whispered, moving closer to Sam instinctively.

"Allen," Penny whispered back. "I do *not* want to talk to him today. He was here for almost two hours last time. He's driving me insane."

"Now, *he's* someone we could ban guilt-free."

"And blacklist ourselves with all the cleaning agencies in the area? There might come a day when we want to use them, Sadie."

"At this point, I wouldn't touch any business he's involved in with a ten-foot pole."

Beside her, Sam signed, *This is the pushy salesman?*

"Yeah," she murmured. "He's the one I told you about, who keeps dropping by to try to convince us to purchase room cleaning services through his agency. No matter how many times we tell him it's too expensive, he just won't take no for an answer."

The door to the laundry room opened and Penny raced over to catch Cody before he made too much noise carrying a full garbage bag out. The four of them stood huddled in the center of the room as Allen tried and failed to open the door before knocking on it.

"Hello, is anyone in there?" he called out. "Your office hours are posted as eight to seven. Hello?"

He kept trying for what had to be a full five minutes before finally giving up. Not daring to peek through the blinds in case he noticed the movement, Sadie pulled her phone out and checked the security cameras to make sure he was actually leaving before she relaxed.

"He's gone," she said. "Thank goodness. Hopefully he doesn't come back this evening."

"It's almost the weekend," Penny said hopefully as she turned the lights back on and unlocked the door. "If we're lucky, we won't see him again until Monday."

While Cody continued bringing the full garbage bags out to the dumpster and Penny went to double check rooms Nine and Ten, Sadie stepped outside with Sam. It was a clear, sunny day, and spring was in full swing. The sun felt nice after being in the cool lobby, but she knew that just a few minutes spent in its glare would leave her sweating.

"Thanks for the flowers, really," she said.

She was still clutching them and hoped he knew how much she meant it. The handpicked bouquet of wildflowers meant much more to her than a bouquet of roses delivered to her by a stranger and ordered through some online service, like her ex had sent her a couple of times back when they were still together and she lived in Lexington. She and Penny hadn't even been in Greencreek for a year, but it felt like everything that had come before was from another lifetime.

Sam smiled in that way that made her chest warm, like he wasn't sure if he was allowed to be happy, then signed, *Do you have time to go on a date this weekend, or will you be too busy with the...* He signed a word she didn't recognize, then fingerspelled it for her. *Vlogger.*

"I won't be babysitting her every second of the day," she said. "I'd love to go out. Maybe Sunday?"

He nodded. Sunday worked. *I'll plan something fun. Do you have work to do?*

"Yeah, I need to bathe some of the dogs," she

said. "I'm glad you stopped by though, and I'm looking forward to Sunday."

She stepped closer to him, careful not to crush the flowers between them as they embraced and shared a lingering kiss. When they were done, she reluctantly waved goodbye and went back into the lobby. She briefly detoured to her upstairs apartment to fill a vase with water, and placed the flowers on the front desk before going through the laundry room and into the kennels.

She was still wearing her scrubs and felt a flush of embarrassment when she realized what a mess she must have looked while Sam was here. She was wearing an unflattering outfit which was covered in dog fur and probably smelled like wet dog to boot, no makeup, and her hair was pulled up in a messy, haphazard bun that she hadn't even checked in the mirror. Unlike Penny, who dressed well and did her hair and makeup first thing every morning, Sadie rarely bothered with any of that until she was done with her kennel chores for the day.

At least Sam worked a physical labor job too, so he understood that work could get messy. He had never complained, or even seemed to notice, but still... maybe she could find some more flattering scrubs online.

At least the dogs didn't care what she wore. Six of the eight kennels were currently full, though two of those were taken up by non-paying residents: Jasper, her own personal dog, a handsome young foxhound, and Angus, an equally handsome border collie who was under her care until his final ownership was legally settled. His previous owner had been murdered, and from what she had heard so far, no one in his immediate family was prepared to take such a high energy, intelligent dog.

Jasper and Angus had quickly become fast friends, so she had put them in neighboring kennels. Rosco, who had been her first ever boarding client, was next in line, then a huge, chubby labrador retriever named Franklin, with gray around his muzzle and an obsession with treats. Next to him was an expensive French bulldog whose owner had sent along individually portioned containers of homemade food for him, and finally there was Loki, another familiar face, a dog she had helped catch after he had gotten lost when his owner was involved in a car crash.

Franklin was getting picked up later today, which meant she was faced with the task of giving him a bath, a new service she offered for an extra fee. A couple of weeks ago, she had gotten lucky and found a large bathing tub and grooming table for sale online in a nearby town. The items were used, but they were in good condition, and they were already earning their keep, even if just because in the raised tub she could give Jasper a bath without the risk of throwing out her back.

The water hookups for the dog bathing tub currently shared the same hookups as one of the washers in the laundry room, which meant only one of them could be running at once and she had to detach the hoses whenever the tub wasn't in use. She already had plans for a whole new grooming room with its own plumbing, but for now that was a far-off, ambitious dream.

She was worried getting Franklin into that tub was an ambitious dream, too. The tub had a ramp, but the big lab didn't want anything to do with it at first, and he was far too heavy for her to lift by herself. It was only with a trail of treats as a lure that she finally managed to get him up and inside the tub. Once he was there, he seemed to relax, and spent the rest of his bath wagging his tail and occasionally shaking water and suds all over her.

She was in the middle of drying him off with a towel when Penny came into the kennel area. The door to the laundry room was propped open with a brick for room for the hose attachment, but she hadn't wanted to set the tub up in the laundry room since she knew bathing the dogs would be a messy endeavor. At least the kennel room had a drain in the floor, and all of the surfaces were epoxied so cleanup was as simple as hosing everything down.

Still, Penny wrinkled her nose when she saw the mess. "Geez, is all of this from one dog?"

"I'm still perfecting my technique," Sadie said. She gave Franklin one final scrub with the towel, then opened his kennel door. He trotted through without any further urging, then went through the rubber door to his outdoor run. She hoped the sun would help dry him off before his owners arrived. She didn't have a proper forced air dryer yet, so she would be stuck with drying him with her own blow dryer if it didn't.

"Well, better you than me," her friend said. "Anyway, we've got a problem."

Her heart sank. Tanisha was supposed to be here in a matter of hours. It was the worst possible time for an issue to crop up.

"What happened?"

"The guest in Room Two?" Penny began. "Her name is Maria, by the way. She says she doesn't have the money to pay for last night. She also says she has nowhere else to go. She offered to clean rooms for us in exchange for a discounted rate, which she *claims* she'd pay us back later."

Sadie winced. Surprisingly, this was the first time they'd had to deal with this issue. It helped that most people paid with a card these days, which made it harder for someone to ditch without paying for their entire stay. They hadn't been too strict on making people who were paying with cash pay up front, and now that was coming back to bite them.

"I'm not sure that's a good idea," she said.

"Me neither. I told her I'd talk to you and think about it, but I'm leaning towards no." Her friend wrinkled her nose. "As bad as that makes me feel to say. She seems really nice, and I saw the room when I went to talk to her, she's been keeping it clean and tidy. I don't think we have to worry about property damage from her."

"If we agreed to let her stay for a lower rate in exchange for help with cleaning, it might cause problems if we end up having to force her out," Sadie said, uncertain.

The thought of forcing someone who had nowhere else to go out of the motel made her feel sick to her stomach, but they couldn't afford to let someone stay indefinitely, for free. Even if Maria kept up her end of the bargain and turned out to do great cleaning work, she wasn't sure they could afford the loss of income right now. Not when they had only just hired Cody.

She could see the same uncertainty in her friend's eyes. The smart business decision would be to tell Maria she had to leave, and to bring Sheriff Islington in to force the issue if she refused. They would have to take last night's unpaid fee as a loss, but in the long run, it would probably end up saving them money.

But she and Penny had always both had bleeding hearts.

"I don't know what to do," her friend admitted.

"Neither do I."

Penny chewed the inside of her cheek. "Do you want to talk to her? She seems trustworthy to me, but I don't know if I want to go with my gut on this. Telling her no would be the smart thing to do."

"Yeah, it would be," Sadie said. "But… I'd like to talk to her, even if all we decide we can do is help her find somewhere else she can stay."

CHAPTER THREE

Sadie didn't get a chance to meet with Maria until nearly an hour later, once she had finished cleaning up after Franklin's bath, changed into clothes that were suitable to wear in public, and did a last-minute touch-up of the lobby.

Once she was satisfied with how it looked, she went out to the parking lot, where Penny was pulling a few brave weeds that had popped up through the cracks in the asphalt since the last time Sam did the yard maintenance around the motel.

"It's too bad we couldn't afford to seal these cracks sooner," Penny said as she tossed the final bundle of weeds into the dumpster.

"That's another thing we need to save up for,"

Sadie said, sighing. "We should ask around town, see if any local businesses can give us a good deal on it."

It was another item to add to their never-ending list. She couldn't worry about it right now—they couldn't afford it at the moment and that wasn't going to change in the next few hours. Trying to put it out of her mind, she followed Penny over to Room Two, where Penny knocked on the door. It opened almost immediately, revealing a middle-aged woman with dark hair and a kind smile. She was pretty, despite the bags under her eyes and the exhaustion on her face.

"Oh, is this the other owner?" she asked when she saw Sadie. "Come in."

She stepped back, welcoming them into the motel room. Penny was right: even though Maria had already been there for a few days, the room was spick and span. She knew it shouldn't matter—heck, whenever *she* stayed in a motel, it always looked like a whirlwind went through right up until the day she left —but it was reassuring to know that Maria wasn't going to cost them money in damages on top of the unpaid night.

"I'm Sadie Barton," Sadie said, extending a hand. Penny had been the one who checked Maria in, and while Sadie had seen her around, she hadn't had a reason to chat with the woman until now.

"Maria Ortega," Maria said. Her handshake was firm, and despite the situation she was in, she didn't look desperate. Hopeful, yes, but like she knew she would be alright no matter what happened. "I already apologized to Penny, but I should apologize to you as well. I had a banking issue pop up unexpectedly. I've never done this before in my life."

"Well, what exactly is the situation?" Sadie asked. "Penny mentioned you can't pay for last night's stay, but that you're hoping you can keep staying here for a discounted rate?"

"In exchange for cleaning the rooms for you, yes," Maria said. "The bank issue should be resolved soon, and once that happens, I can pay you for last night and whatever else I owe you. I think I already mentioned I'm interested in paying a weekly rate, if that's something you offer. I understand that after this, you'll probably want me to pay in advance, which I should be able to manage. It's looking like I might be here long term, and there aren't many other options in the area."

For a moment, Sadie was tempted to suggest she go stay at Loretta Browning's bed-and-breakfast, but if Maria couldn't pay, then she couldn't pay, and Sadie doubted Loretta's prices were lower than theirs. Besides, Loretta seemed like she might be more than a little crazy, and she felt bad at the idea of subjecting the other woman to that.

Maria didn't seem like the sort of person who would skip out on them, but going with a gut feeling on something like this was risky business.

"I'm sure we can work something out for last night, either way," Penny said. "I think Sadie and I are going to have to take some more time to discuss everything else, though."

Sadie nodded. "Sometimes things happen, we get that, and like Penny said, we're willing to work with you on a night or two. But we've never had a long-term guest before, and even if you could pay everything upfront, right now, there would be a few things we'd have to look into first."

She wanted to ask more, to ask why Maria was in this position, why she so desperately needed to stay in Greencreek, but she didn't want to pry. As long as Maria didn't cause trouble at the motel and paid what she owed sooner rather than later, the rest wasn't their business.

"I'll need time to arrange for something else if I have to be out by tonight," Maria began. The sound of a vehicle pulling into the parking lot distracted Sadie. She glanced over her shoulder, then did a double take when she saw a pristine white cargo van pull in. It was the exact same make and model as the vehicle Tanisha had registered when she reserved her rooms. She nudged Penny, whose eyes widened when she saw it.

"Are they here early? Shoot, are we ready?"

"I think so," Sadie whispered back. "You checked Rooms Nine and Ten and I just finished tidying the lobby." She glanced around the parking lot and up and down the row of rooms. Everything looked as good as it was going to get. "I think we're ready."

Penny turned back to Maria. "I'm so sorry, but we're going to have to come back to this conversation later. If we don't let you know by..." She trailed off and glanced at Sadie. "Three or four? Then you can assume you're fine to stay another night and we'll try to work something out with you in the morning."

"Oh, thank you so much," Maria said. "I appreciate you even taking the time to think about this."

Sadie still felt uncertain as Maria shut the door and they turned to greet Tanisha. Letting her stay longer and accepting her offer of labor in exchange for a lowered rate seemed like a recipe for disaster, but her conscience was tugging at her.

She wasn't sure if letting Maria stay another night without coming to an agreement was a good idea, but she didn't blame Penny for her self-imposed deadline.

It wouldn't be fair to leave Maria uncertain of where she was going to sleep until the very last moment. Besides, they had more important things to deal with. Mainly, making sure Tanisha and her videographer had the best stay possible.

"Whoo, we're here!"

The young woman who got out of the van looked like she was around Sadie and Penny's age. Her curly black hair was pulled back from her face, and she was in full tourist mode with a waist pack, a tank top that read "Georgia" across the front of it, and brightly colored flip-flops. Sadie heard the door on the other side slam shut, and a moment later a second woman joined them. Her mousy brown hair was pulled back into a short ponytail, and she had a professional and expensive looking video camera in hand, which she panned across the parking lot before focusing on Tanisha, who smiled brightly at it and waved.

"Hi, everyone, we made it! This is the infamous Sit, Stay, Sleep Motel and Boarding located on Highway 78 in Georgia, near the tiny town of Greencreek. We're going to be spending the week here, exploring the local area and providing all of you with a very thorough review on the motel and its amenities. I heard it doubles as a boarding kennel and dog training center, so if we're lucky, you might be seeing some furry faces and wagging tails in this week's video!"

She spotted Sadie and Penny approaching from across the parking lot and turned toward them. Her videographer turned the camera in their direction as well. Sadie felt a prickle of unease at the thought of being filmed, but she had known what they were getting into. She was just going to have to make peace with the fact that thousands of people were going to watch her going about her daily life for the next week.

"Are you the owners?" Tanisha asked, striding across the parking lot to meet them halfway.

"Good guess," Penny said. "I'm Penny Montgomery, and this is my best friend and business partner, Sadie Barton. We co-own Sit, Stay, Sleep Motel and Boarding."

"I'm Tanisha Verdan," she said, shaking first Penny's hand, then Sadie's. "And over here is my videographer, Emily Hubert. She's the real magic behind the channel—you might even call her my lucky charm."

Emily looked embarrassed but pleased at the praise, though she didn't let it distract her from doing her job. She held the camera steady as Tanisha spoke.

"Well, it's lovely to meet you both," Penny said.

"If you'd like to follow us into the lobby, we'll get you checked in and hand over your room keys."

"Do you mind if I ask you some questions about the history of the motel while we have you?" Tanisha asked as they moved toward the lobby door.

"Not at all," Penny said.

She looked like she was in her element, and for the first time, Sadie realized her friend had put extra effort into her hair and makeup today. She was wearing a nice pair of dark slacks and a deep red blouse, nicer clothes than she usually wore for an average workday. She flipped her hair over her shoulder as she turned what Sadie knew she considered the good side of her face toward the camera, her heels clacking on the ground.

Sadie narrowed her eyes. This reminded her of that time in middle school when they did the Wizard of Oz play together. Penny had been cripplingly shy back then, but as soon as she got on the stage, it was like she was a different person entirely.

"Do you know how old the building is and when it originally opened? From what I understand, the two of you reopened the motel under its new name back in August of last year. Is that correct?"

"That's right," Penny said. As to when the

building was built, she glanced towards Sadie. "Do you remember what Walter said?"

"I don't even know if *he* knows exactly when it was built," Sadie said, wracking her mind. She felt put on the spot. Why hadn't she thought to do some more research before Tanisha arrived? "But I do know it had been open for decades, though not all of it is original…"

She and Penny filled Tanisha in on as much of the motel's history as they could as they finished the process of checking them in. When they handed them the room keys, Tanisha glanced down at hers excitedly.

"Oh great, you remembered! Not to sound morbid, but Room Ten is where those murders happened a couple years back, right?"

"That's right," Penny said. She sounded uncertain, as if she wasn't sure whether Tanisha was viewing this as a selling point or something to be concerned about. "All of the rooms have been completely redone since then."

"Good to know," Tanisha said with a laugh as she pocketed the key. "I won't have anything to worry about except for ghosts. Oh, before we get too far, can I have you sign these release forms? The forms give us permission to film on the property and to use the footage for commercial purposes. We'll leave extra forms for your employees to sign, and if anyone *doesn't* want to be filmed, all they have to do is tell us and we'll either keep the camera off them entirely, or if that's impossible, we'll blur their faces in our footage. And if there's anywhere you don't want us to film, just let us know and I'll make a note of that, or Emily will. I know how intrusive this sort of thing can feel, so we try to be as respectful as possible."

Sadie quickly read through the form Emily handed her, saw that it said what Tanisha said it did, and signed it. Penny did the same, and they accepted an extra form for Cody.

"You're welcome to film anywhere you want on the property, but I want to ask that you don't film any of our other guests, or their rooms, without getting permission from them first," Sadie said. "Oh, and if you go around back, you'll see a row of outdoor dog runs. You can film them from a distance, but please don't get too close to the runs. I don't want the dogs to get too stressed."

"Got it," Tanisha said. "The last thing we'd want to do is frighten any poor puppies. Now, as for Greencreek itself, can you recommend any must-see locations, or any awesome local businesses we should support?"

"Sunshine Desserts," Penny said. "Bailey, the owner, she makes the best cookies I've ever had in my life. You have to stop there."

"Ooh, Emily, make a note of it," Tanisha said. "This is *exactly* why I love filming travel vlogs in these tiny, out-of-the-way locations. Each one has its own hidden gem."

It seemed Tanisha was in the right profession, because she could keep a conversation going for a long time without it feeling strained and never seemed to run out of questions to ask. It wasn't until Cody came back in, froze, and gave the camera a wide-eyed look that Tanisha finally said, "Oops, I've been talking your ears off, haven't I? I think it's time for Emily and I to settle into our rooms. Thank you so much for letting us do this. I can't *wait* to post this vlog next week and help your lovely motel get all of the attention it deserves."

CHAPTER FOUR

A thump and a crash woke Sadie early the next morning. She sat upright in bed and rubbed the sleep from her eyes to see two shapes wrestling on the floor.

"Cut it out, you two," she croaked.

The two dogs separated and trotted over to the bed to stand side by side, looking up at her, their heads cocked at the exact same angle. Angus's black and white coat had a string of slobber on it, and Jasper's white-tipped tail was a blur behind him.

She scowled, not so easily won over by their cute expressions. "What time is it, anyway?," she murmured, reaching for her phone.

It was six forty-five... only fifteen minutes until her alarm was supposed to go off. With a sigh, she flopped back down onto her pillow. The mattress dipped as Jasper put his front feet on the bed and pressed his cold nose against her face.

She groaned and turned on her side, but he persisted, snuffling her ear. Finally giving in, she turned back over and scratched his chin.

"You're a menace," she murmured. "Both of you. Is it too much to ask to sleep until seven? Really?"

Over by the bedroom door, Angus turned in a tight circle and let out a single, high-pitched bark—his sign that he needed to go outside. With a groan, she dragged herself out of bed and let them out of the bedroom. Both dogs raced over to the door that led down to the lobby. Angus had been with her for over a month by this point and was very familiar with her routine and seemed to be enjoying his stay with her.

A part of her hoped the legal matters surrounding his ownership would be cleared up soon, because she knew the longer she had him, the harder it was going to be to let him go. Already, she was tempted to keep him if none of his previous owners' friends or family was willing to take him in, but she knew she wouldn't be able to give him what he deserved. Not really.

He was young, energetic, and incredibly intelligent, and she had her hands full with Jasper and her dog training business. It wouldn't be fair to Jasper to put him on the sidelines because she adopted a new and demanding young dog. Jasper was her demo dog and took part in every class she hosted. If she split that time with Angus, her poor foxhound would have even less space in her busy life.

No, Angus deserved to go to someone who would have the time and energy to dedicate to his training and either make him into a great sport dog or a herding dog, like his original owners had intended, and Jasper deserved her focus and attention.

She shuffled downstairs in her slippers and let herself into the kennel room, where she was greeted by a cacophony of barks as the boarding dogs woke up. She put Jasper and Angus into their kennels at the end of the row, then began opening the sliding barriers to the outside runs one by one. While the dogs went outside to do their business, she went back upstairs, still yawning, to attend to her own morning routine.

She was waiting for her coffee to percolate and scrolling through her phone's notifications when she spotted something unusual. There was a single *Person Detected* notification from the security camera app. She usually left notifications off for the cameras at the front of the motel, since with all of the people coming and going her phone would be chiming constantly, so this notification could only have come from the single outdoor camera in the back, which overlooked the outdoor dog runs.

Curious, she clicked the notification and reviewed the video. The ghostly black-and-white footage showed two people walking through the grass toward the woodsTanisha and Emily. They didn't go near the dog kennels, though they did pause to film the building from a distance before continuing into the trees. More than a little puzzled, Sadie watched as they vanished into the darkness.

It wasn't that she had a problem with them going into the woods at night. Though, from a liability standpoint, it seemed like a bad idea, she just couldn't understand *why* they would want to. What could they possibly want to film for their vlog in a dark forest in the middle of the night?

Confused and a little worried, she checked the rest of the footage from last night to make sure they had gotten back safely. Thankfully, they returned to their rooms an hour later and looked none the worse for wear.

Deciding to trust that they knew what they were doing, she didn't know the first thing about filming a vlog. After all, she shrugged and put it out of her mind. It was a Saturday, which meant she had other things to focus on. Days off were a thing of the past, and Saturdays were usually one of her busiest days since that was when she offered private lessons.

Today's client was a tiny chihuahua mix. The little dog had come from a hoarder's home and had never once been outside the house until she was rescued and then adopted by her new owners. As a result, she was terrified of almost everything. This was the third time she would be meeting with the dog and her owners, and she was eager to see the progress they had made since their last lesson.

She checked the time. It was a little after seven, and she should have just enough time to finish her morning kennel chores before meeting the dog's owners at ten.

Despite her best intentions, she ended up running a little late and was in a hurry by the time she left. As she raced out the lobby door, she bumped smack dab into Hunter Underwood, the young man who delivered cookies to the motel from Sunshine Desserts a few times a week. They resold the cookies to their guests, and despite the small markup, they went through them surprisingly quickly.

Hunter was standing just outside the lobby door, looking distractedly down the row of motel rooms. After apologizing for bumping into him, Sadie followed his gaze and spotted Tanisha and Emily filming in front of their room.

"What's going on there?" he asked her.

"Tanisha's a guest who does travel vlogs," Sadie explained. "She's going to be filming around Greencreek all week. I mentioned Sunshine Desserts, so you and Bailey might see her there."

A glint entered his eye. "So, she wants to interview locals? I could tell them all about the motel and the crazy things that have happened here."

Sadie narrowed her eyes. "You can talk to them if you want, but stick to the facts, Hunter. Don't go spreading rumors. We're hoping to get more business from this. We don't need bad publicity chasing potential guests away."

"Right, of course," he said distractedly, still gazing at the two women. "Facts."

She gave him a distrustful look, but she had to get going, so she had no choice but to leave him to it.

CHAPTER FIVE

As Sadie drove back to the motel after her private lesson, she was awash with a sense of pride and accomplishment. The little Chihuahua mix, named Soda, was improving in leaps and bounds. Instead of cowering in her crate, which her owners had turned into a cozy cave she could come and go from whenever she wanted, she had tentatively come out to sniff Sadie's shoes when she arrived. She had even began accepting treats while Sadie was there, a huge accomplishment. She knew it would be a long time before the little dog could live a normal life, but she was confident they would get there.

She was so distracted by her mental review of the great training lesson that she was already turning into the parking lot when she spotted the vehicle. *Allen.*

She was tempted to turn right back around and leave again, but he had already spotted her and was waving.

Reluctantly, she pulled into a parking space and got out of her SUV. Allen made a beeline toward her, a look of determination on his face. Looking past him, she could see Penny talking animatedly to Tanisha and Emily through the lobby window. In the other direction, she saw Maria going into Room Eight with a cleaning cart.

She narrowed her eyes. Had Penny gone ahead and accepted the deal? She felt like it was the sort of thing they should have decided together, but then, she *had* been gone for most of the morning.

"Sadie," Allen said with a too-wide grin on his face, "I'm so glad I caught you. Ms. Penny is busy with some other guests, and I was just about to give up and come back later when I spotted you."

Great, she thought. *If only I was a few minutes later.* She forced a polite smile on her face, though, and said, "I'm afraid I've got some things I have to take care of too, Allen. We still aren't ready to hire a cleaning service. We have your card, so we'll keep you in mind if we decide that's the direction we want to go in the future."

"I'm quite certain we can find a plan that works

for you. If you'd just let me take a look in one of the motel rooms—"

"I'm sorry, but I'm really not comfortable with that," Sadie said, her patience beginning to wear thin.

"Well, I understand that you and Penny do all the cleaning by yourselves. Which is very admirable, of course, but if you're not professional cleaners, I can guarantee there's a *lot* you're missing. If I could just take a look, I could point out some areas that are commonly missed by amateurs–"

"We're not interested right now," Sadie said firmly, interrupting him. "I'm sorry, but I really have to go. The dogs need me."

It was a bald-faced lie. She had checked them on the cameras before driving home, and they were all doing fine. Maybe they should just give in and ban him from the property. It might cause problems down the road, but she didn't know how else to make him leave them alone. Maybe he kept coming back because he thought their politeness was a sign of indecision.

Snapping at him might help, actually, but she felt a little bad for him. He looked exhausted and stressed, and she couldn't imagine a job as a door-to-door salesman was easy, especially out here in what was a relatively poor area of the state. But she wasn't about to sign up for a service she didn't need just because she felt bad for him.

"Just give me five minutes—"

"We aren't interested," she repeated. "Goodbye, Allen. I have to get to work."

Without giving him a chance to speak, she turned and began rapidly striding toward the lobby, but she paused and changed directions when Maria came out of Room Eight to get a spray cleaner from the cleaning cart.

"Hey, Maria?" she said. "Can you come with me for a second? I'd like to speak with you and Penny." She glanced over her shoulder. "And if Allen thinks you work here, he's going to start hassling you, so it might be best if you hide out in the lobby, anyway."

"Oh." Maria looked worried but put the cleaning spray down and pulled the door most of the way shut behind her. "Sure."

Penny, Tanisha, and Emily all looked up when she and Maria stepped through the lobby door. Her friend looked relieved to see her.

"Oh, good, you're back," Penny said. "We might have an issue."

Sadie's stomach sank. "What is it?"

"It's probably nothing…" Emily hedged. She was holding the camera, but it was pointed at the floor.

"No, Emily, you heard something," Tanisha said. "I believe you."

"You... heard something?" Sadie asked, confused.

"Emily says she heard something in the room next to hers last night," Penny explained. "Room Eight."

"I thought it was a person at first," Emily said. "But now I'm not sure. Tanisha thought it might have been rats, but I don't know... it sounded really strange. I heard what sounded like scratching on the other side of the wall, but it was something *big*. I know what mice sound like, and it wasn't that. Then I heard..." She hesitated, her expression uncertain and a little frightened. "I heard a moan, like someone was in pain, but maybe that was just the wind." She looked doubtful. There hadn't been any wind last night. "I don't know, it was really creepy."

"There wasn't anyone in Room Eight last night," Sadie said. She glanced over at Maria with a frown. The room had been cleaned when the guest who had been staying there left two days ago, so why was Maria cleaning it again?

"I know," Penny said. "I went to check it and didn't see any signs of a disturbance."

"It was probably some sort of animal," Tanisha said, though she didn't look as sure as she sounded. She gave an uncomfortable smile before adding,

"Either that or ghosts, and I like to think I'm a skeptic."

"Well, thanks for letting us know what you heard," Sadie said. "Did you want us to put you in a different room, Emily? I think Room One is empty right now. That would put you far away from Room Eight."

"No, it's okay," Emily said. "We just wanted to let you know."

"If you guys *do* figure out what the noise was, I'd love it if you let us know," Tanisha added. "But it's probably nothing."

Sadie watched them leave the lobby, worry gnawing at her. If they *did* have rats, getting an exterminator was going to be expensive.

She glanced at Maria. "Do you mind waiting in here for a second? I need to speak with Penny privately."

"Of course," Maria said, making her way over to one of the uncomfortable chairs across from the front desk. "Go ahead. "

Sadie pulled Penny into the laundry room.

"Why was Maria cleaning Room Eight?" she asked, keeping her voice low so it wouldn't travel through the door. "Did you agree to let her stay in exchange for cleaning?"

"Look, she overheard Tanisha and Emily complaining about the noises," Penny said. "Maria offered to give the room a thorough cleaning and check for any signs of rodents or other pests. She said she used to work for a housekeeping service, and I figured having the room get a once-over by a professional couldn't hurt."

"So, are we letting her stay in exchange for cleaning services, then?" Sadie asked.

"I don't know," Penny said. "I meant for it to be a one-off... maybe a way for her to pay for Thursday night or last night's stay. Do you want me to tell her not to do it?"

"I don't know," Sadie muttered. She felt a headache coming on. "Let's just ask her to hold off for an hour or two for now. I still need to check the laws to see if there's any way we can land ourselves in hot water with this."

Penny nodded, looking worried. "I'll tell her. Sorry for not talking to you first."

"It's fine," Sadie said. "I get why you did. If we do have rats or mice, we need to know."

"I need to go to the bank before they close for the weekend," Penny said. "Will you have time to do the research while I'm gone? I don't want to leave her hanging in uncertainty for too long."

"All right," Sadie said. "I'll text you whatever I find out."

She returned to the lobby and stood in the entrance to wave as Penny left. Allen's vehicle was still in the parking lot, she noticed, but she didn't see him anywhere. For now, she was just going to count her lucky stars that he was actually giving her the space she had asked for.

She told Maria that she needed to double check a few things before they made the arrangement official, and the other woman agreed to take a break and wait in her motel room for a little while. Sadie settled in behind the front desk to begin doing her research. It took her a while to find anything pertinent, but after over half an hour of searching and doublechecking employment and housing laws, she was satisfied that they could let Maria stay and work in exchange for a room without any issues, as long as she stayed for fewer than thirty days.

Having someone to take the cleaning load off of the two of them would be nice. Maybe Allen was getting to her, because she was becoming more and more paranoid that they weren't doing a good enough job of cleaning by themselves. If they really had rats, then there was clearly something they were missing.

When she knocked on Maria's door to tell her the good news, the other woman looked deeply relieved.

"Oh, thank you so much," she said. "I'll get right back to cleaning Room Eight, and I'll let you know if I see any evidence of pests. I heard what that girl was telling Penny. To me, it sounds like it might have been something larger than a rat. Have you checked the attic for ingress from squirrels or raccoons?"

"We did when we first began working on the place," Sadie admitted, "but that was almost a year ago."

"It might be smart to check again," Maria said. "Squirrels and raccoons can be menaces. They love nesting in attics. We had some flying squirrels in the attic while I was growing up, and when they ran around, it sounded like someone was walking up there."

"Hopefully that's it. I'd rather evict a couple of squirrels than have to deal with rats," Sadie said. She remembered what Tanisha said, and added, "Or ghosts."

She returned to the lobby, glad they had worked the issue with Maria out, even though she still wasn't sure it was the smartest idea. She had her phone in her hand and was about to text Penny with an update when she heard an ear-piercing scream from outside.

Racing out of the lobby, she saw Maria standing in front of the door to Room Eight. A white fog — or was it smoke? — billowed from the open door, and Maria's face was as pale as snow as she stared inside.

"What happened?" Sadie asked as she raced over. Her first worry was that the room was on fire, but what Maria said turned out to be even worse..

"There's a man inside," Maria said, pointing with a shaking finger. "And I think he's dead."

CHAPTER SIX

Sadie stood in the doorway to Room Eight, staring at the familiar form that lay on the neatly made bed. *This* was where Allen had gone. His eyes were closed and he looked peaceful, as if he was sleeping. In fact, she wasn't entirely convinced that he *wasn't* sleeping. She took a step through the doorway, then hesitated as the strange white fog billowed around her.

It didn't have a strong smell, and it definitely wasn't smoke, but she had no idea where it was coming from. She looked at Allen again, staring at his chest through the mist as she waited for a sign that he was breathing.

His chest remained still. She hesitated for a second longer, then stepped back out of the room. Her conscience and common sense were at war with each other. If Allen was dead, then there was a good chance it was this strange fog that had killed him.

She turned to Maria. "Quick," she said, "do you have something I could wrap around my face? A hand towel or scarf?"

"Yes, I can go get a towel from my room."

"Wet it down for me," Sadie requested. "I'm going to use it to try to get through this fog safely, so I can check on Allen."

Maria hurried away, and Sadie, whose cell phone was still clutched in her hand, dialed 911.

When Maria returned, she had two damp towels with her. Sadie accepted one and gave her the phone in return, so Maria could continue the conversation with the dispatcher. Folding the towel in half, Sadie pressed it over her mouth and nose and stepped into the room. She squinted her eyes, hoping the fog wouldn't blind her.

Through the wall, she could faintly hear the sound of a movie playing from Room Nine. Emily must have been in her room. Had she been caught up in whatever was going on?

Working quickly, she shook Allen's shoulder. There was no response. She pressed her fingers first to his neck and then to the inside of his wrist, searching for a pulse. She couldn't find one, and she hadn't seen a sign of life since she first looked into the room. She glanced back toward the doorway, torn. She needed to go check on Emily and the other guests, but she didn't want to leave him in here. Someone needed to start CPR on him as soon as possible. If he could be saved, then they were running out of time.

Just as she was about to hurry back outside, Maria hurried in, the second towel wrapped around her face. Without saying a word, she gestured at Allen's feet, then looped her arms under his shoulders. Sadie grabbed his ankles, and they heaved him out of the room together. After laying him gently on the sidewalk, Maria dropped the towel to the ground and picked the cell phone up from where she had set it down.

"Okay, we have him," she said. "What now?"

"Now you're going to start CPR..." the dispatcher said over speaker.

While Maria was busy trying to save Allen's life, Sadie hurried to Room Nine and pounded on the door. It took a second, but soon enough it opened a crack and Emily blinked out at her.

"Did you figure out what that noise was?"

"Are you okay?" Sadie asked, ignoring her question.

She pushed the door open unceremoniously, making the other woman stumble back a little, and looked around the room. There was no sign of the fog, just the quiet hum of a fan the other woman had set up on the floor next to her bed, which Emily stooped to turn off. Her laptop was open on the desk, a movie paused part way through—no, not a movie, Sadie realized. Emily must have been editing some of the footage she had been recording.

"You need to get out *now*," Sadie said. "There's—" She hesitated, not sure what to call it. "Some sort of gas leak, I think. One of the other guests already fell victim to it. The police are on their way. I need everyone to wait in the parking lot."

Emily's eyes widened. Before she could get drawn into answering questions, Sadie hurried to Room Ten and gave the same warning to Tanisha, who hurried outside in a panic.

By the time Sadie finished evacuating the other two guests and made sure the dogs were all locked outside in their runs, in case whatever was going on somehow affected the kennels as well, she could hear sirens.

Help arrived a few seconds later. By then, that white fog had stopped billowing out of the room, but

Allen still lay motionless and unresponsive on the ground.

The paramedics got there first and rushed over to him. Maria, who had been trying to save him this entire time, backed away to stand next to Sadie. She was pale and her hands were shaking.

"What happened?" she whispered. "Do you think he had a heart attack?"

"I have no idea," Sadie said. She thought about how Allen had looked earlier that day: tired and stressed. Maybe he *had* had a heart attack, and the weird fog was just... a coincidence? It didn't seem likely, but it was the less frightening option.

Her attention focused on Sheriff Islington's patrol vehicle when he pulled into the parking lot. He gave Sadie a nod as he got out of his vehicle, but made his way over to the paramedics first, to speak with them as they examined Allen and began to load him onto a stretcher.

While the paramedics worked, he glanced into the motel room, then walked over to Sadie and Maria. "What happened?" he asked without any preamble.

Sadie told him everything; the scream, the white fog, using the damp towels to go into the room, Maria helping her carry Allen out. He listened intently, then began asking questions.

"When was the last time you saw this guest alive?"

"He's not a guest," she corrected. "He wasn't even supposed to be in there. He's a salesman who keeps trying to get us to sign up for a company that provides a cleaning service to businesses in the area."

The sheriff raised an eyebrow. "So, he was trespassing?"

She supposed he was, technically, since she had very clearly told him she didn't want him going into the rooms, but it didn't feel right to say anything bad about him, not with how still Allen was as the paramedics loaded the stretcher into the ambulance.

"Yes," she said reluctantly. "Is he…"

The sheriff gave a brief shake of his head. "They've already called it. I'm sorry."

"This is all my fault," Maria moaned, clutching her chest.

"I'm afraid I didn't catch your name," Sheriff Islington said.

"Maria Ortega," she said. "This is horrible. He would still be alive if it wasn't for me."

The sheriff glanced at Sadie, then looked back at Maria, suspicion dawning on his face.

CHAPTER SEVEN

"Can you elaborate on that for me?"

"I didn't close the door all the way," Maria explained in a tremulous voice. "I was in the middle of cleaning the room, and I thought I'd be coming right back, so I didn't latch it. If I hadn't left the door open, he wouldn't have been able to go in, and then none of this would have happened."

"Are you an employee of the motel?" Sheriff Islington asked as he noted the information down.

Maria shook her head, then said, "Not quite."

"She's doing some cleaning for us in exchange for a discounted rate," Sadie explained.

"I see. Do you remember which chemicals you were using to clean? Did you see any sign of the fog or smoke in the room while you were cleaning it?"

Maria hesitated. She looked over at Sadie, and a guilty expression flashed across her face before she turned back to the sheriff. "I'm sorry, but I didn't see any fog. I'm not sure what Sadie's talking about."

Sadie gaped at her. The blatant lie stung, all the more for being such a surprise.

"What are you talking about?" she asked. "You were right there. You saw it too."

Maria shook her head. "I'm sorry. I opened the door and saw a man on the bed when he wasn't supposed to be there. That's why I screamed. I didn't see anything unnatural."

Sheriff Islington lowered his pen and notepad slowly, looking back and forth between the two women. "Well, now that's a puzzle," he said. He focused on Sadie. "Are you feeling well? Is it possible the victim was smoking in the room prior to his passing?"

"He wasn't smoking," Sadie said, more than a little offended. "We'd be able to smell it if he was, these are all no-smoking rooms. And I know what I saw. It was a heavy fog, not a few puffs of cigarette smoke. When I first saw it from a distance, I thought the entire room was on fire."

He turned back to Maria. "And you're quite certain you didn't see anything?"

Maria shook her head. "I'm sorry. I'm sure Sadie believes what she says she saw – I'm not trying to accuse her of lying. I can only speak as to what I saw, and I didn't see anything, sir."

"You did," Sadie insisted. "Why are you lying?"

Maria gave her an uncomfortable look. "I'm sorry, but I'm telling the truth."

"Let's all take a deep breath and try to move on," the sheriff said. "I still have more questions. We can return to the fog later."

Sadie answered the rest of his questions about Allen and how well she knew him with a clenched jaw. When he finished, she asked, "Do you think we should close the motel until we figure out what's going on?"

"At this point, I'm going to say no," the sheriff said. "We have no evidence his death was anything besides natural causes. I think it would be overkill to shut your business down."

"What about the fog?" she asked. "What if it's something that happens to another room?"

Sheriff Islington hesitated, and in that moment she realized he didn't believe her. "Let me see if I can get to the bottom of this. You two hang tight. I'll ask if anyone else remembers seeing this fog."

Sadie didn't want to stand next to Maria while she

waited, so she walked a few feet away and leaned against the wall of the motel, her arms crossed over her chest. She watched as Sheriff Islington spoke to Tanisha, Emily, and the other two guests. All of them shook their heads, and he had a worried look on his face when he came back over to her.

"I'm sorry, Sadie. None of them remember seeing anything, though they admit they were in a hurry when they left their rooms. I don't mean to pry, but when's the last time you saw a doctor?"

He was worried about her. He thought she was insane or sick — but not that she was telling the truth.

"I'm healthy," she muttered, "and I know what I saw."

His lips pressed together. "Do you have working smoke and carbon monoxide detectors in each room?"

She nodded.

"Did any of them go off?"

She shook her head.

"I see. As part of the investigation, I'll be going through and checking all of them, but for now just cordon off Room Eight – I don't want any guests or employees going inside until I get a chance to thoroughly search it. Is Penny around?"

"She's in town," Sadie said, her shoulders stiff. "I'll call her."

"Do that," he said. "We'll get to the bottom of this, and I hope I'll be able to put your mind at ease soon."

CHAPTER EIGHT

"She's lying for some reason, and the worst part is, it worked. Sheriff Islington didn't believe me. You do, right?"

Sadie was leaning against the front desk, her arms crossed as she glared at Penny and Sam. Sheriff Islington and the ambulance had left over an hour ago—as had two of their guests. Right now, Tanisha, Emily, and Maria were the only ones who insisted on staying. Sadie wasn't sure she was comfortable with that, and she definitely didn't want to see either of them get hurt, but Tanisha had been insistent, and Sadie doubted herself just enough that she hadn't put her foot down.

Sam nodded. She didn't see any doubt in his eyes, and something in her chest relaxed slightly. Penny hesitated a moment longer, but then she nodded as well.

"I *do*, but why would she lie?"

"I don't know," Sadie said. "The only explanation I can think of is that she had something to do with it."

"But why?" her friend asked. "I mean, *we* don't like Allen, but Maria wouldn't have any reason to want to hurt him."

"As far as we know," Sadie said. "How much do we really know about her? About either of them? What if Allen wasn't even a salesman? For all we know, they go way back."

Did the fog have a smell? Sam signed. *A taste? Did it leave any residue on your skin or clothes after you went through it?*

Sadie shook her head. "No. Well, no to the residue and the smell. I had a wet towel over my face, and I wasn't breathing through my mouth, so I couldn't tell you if it had a taste. It didn't seem like a good idea to breathe it in."

Smart. He looked worried. *Did you get a chance to ask Maria why she lied, after the sheriff left?*

Penny looked between them, clearly trying and failing to figure out what Sam was saying. She understood a few basic signs by this point but hadn't studied with him as extensively as Sadie had.

"I tried, but she locked herself in her room," Sadie said. "We should kick her out. I don't want her to stay here if she's not going to be honest."

"We *just* told her she could stay," Penny said. "I agree it's suspicious, but I don't know if kicking her out is the right thing to do."

"Why not?" Sadie asked, pushing away from the desk to pace across the room. "She lied to the *police*, Penny."

"Maybe," her friend said, "or maybe she's not sure about *what* she saw."

Sadie stopped dead. "I thought you said you believe me."

"I do," Penny said quickly. "I completely believe that you think you saw fog coming out of the room."

"That I *think* I saw?" Sadie said. She crossed her arms again, feeling defensive. "You don't believe I *actually* saw it?"

"I don't know what I think," Penny admitted. "Did you check the security cameras?"

"Of course," Sadie said. "I gave Sheriff Islington all of today's footage."

"And could you see fog on the footage?"

Sadie pressed her lips together. "It's hard to see. The camera is at an angle to look into the rooms. It catches the doors at an oblique angle, and it was sunny out. There's maybe a few wisps of something, but whatever the fog was, it evaporated quickly in the sunlight and fresh air."

Penny gave her a worried look that mirrored the look Sheriff Islington had given her earlier.

"Let's try to talk to Maria in the morning," she said. "We've all had a long, stressful day. Do you want to take the rest of the night off? I'm happy to watch the lobby for the rest of the evening if you want to spend some time with the dogs."

"Yeah, I think I'll do that," Sadie said, her voice tight. Penny's doubt stung even worse than Maria's lie did. She knew her friend was worried about her, but she felt like she was going crazy. She needed someone to believe she wasn't crazy. She glanced at Sam, wondering if he had the same doubts that Penny did.

If he did, he didn't say anything about it. He just signed, *Want some company?*

She nodded, feeling some of the tension ease out of her shoulders. "Yeah, that would be nice."

CHAPTER NINE

Walking with Sam and the dogs helped her feel better, but only a little. She still couldn't believe Maria had lied to Sheriff Islington, but what hurt even more was that no one, not even her best friend, seemed to believe her.

Oh, she knew Penny didn't think she was *lying,* But she didn't believe Sadie had truly seen what she said she saw. Sam did, though, and his faith in her helped even more than the soothing presence of the dogs did.

They walked the boarding dogs two at a time, each of them taking charge of one leash, and when they were done, she walked Angus and Jasper back to Sam's house, so he could get Briar and Rose, his two red coonhounds. They ended the evening by taking the four dogs on a long walk, stopping off at the old, overgrown flower garden by the decaying shed where, months ago, Sadie had found a buried skeleton. Perhaps that discovery should have scared her off from the area, but despite the history of the place, the little glade was peaceful.

The woman who had been buried here was the one who had planted and tended to the garden, and the love the woman had for her flowers, which still grew nearly two decades later, seemed to linger in the secluded space. Sadie liked to come here sometimes to just sit with Jasper. She found it relaxing, and that evening was no different.

By the time she returned to the motel, she wasn't mad at Penny anymore. Not really. She wasn't sure whether she would believe someone who claimed to have seen ghostly fog that no one else did. For a second, she felt a chill but told herself she was being ridiculous. She didn't believe in ghosts, and that wasn't about to change just because she had seen some mysterious fog. There had to be a reasonable explanation behind it.

The next morning came with no new updates, and thankfully, no more fatalities either.

She spotted Tanisha and Emily heading into town bright and early, and Maria joined them in the lobby as soon as Penny unlocked the door. Sadie, who was in her scrubs and already partway through her kennel chores, took a short break to converse with the two women. Maria avoided her gaze and focused on Penny as she spoke.

"What would you like me to do today? Are there any other rooms that need cleaning?"

"Rooms Four and Six," Penny said. "I didn't clean them after our guests left early yesterday, so you can get started on those. Do you still think your bank issue will be cleared up in a couple of days?"

"I'll speak to them on Monday," Maria said. "But the teller I spoke to on Friday seemed hopeful that it would be resolved by then. I'll pay you what I owe you, minus the hours for my labor."

"Sounds fair to me," Penny said.

Sadie scowled. Before, she had been okay with the women staying here or at least hadn't minded Maria's presence on a personal level even if she thought it was a bad business decision. She knew that Penny thought Maria was telling the truth about not seeing the fog, and so she had no reason to kick her out, and if Sadie pushed then *she* would be the bad guy.

Penny must have sensed her sour mood because she said, "You've still got that lunch date with Sam today, right? I'll take care of things in here until you get back, if you want."

Right, her date with Sam. She had completely forgotten, not that she would ever tell him that. In her defense, a lot had happened since they arranged the date on Friday.

"Fine," Sadie said stiffly. Relenting slightly, she added, "I'll try to be back by early afternoon, so you can take some time off too."

She finished the kennel chores in plenty of time to get ready for her date with Sam. She was glad for an opportunity to dress up a little so, for once, she didn't feel like a ragamuffin while she was out with him. He picked her up just before noon and they headed into town together.

It was a nice day, so they decided to eat outside. After picking up their Chinese takeout from the little takeout place just outside of town, Sam drove them to a wooded park on the outskirts of town, and they settled in to eat.

The discussion, at first, centered around Allen. With no new updates, and no flood of safety inspectors coming to shut down the motel, Sadie felt like they were in limbo.

Maybe his death was from natural causes, Sam signed, putting down his chopsticks to do so. *It makes sense. He saw that the door wasn't shut properly and went into the room. If something happened like a stroke or heart attack, maybe he was struck with fatigue and decided to lay down, only to never open his eyes again.*

"I want to believe that," Sadie said, poking at her lo mein with her chopsticks. "But what about the fog? That has to be related."

Sam shrugged. *The world is full of mysteries,* he signed. *I've seen things I can't explain out here.*

"Are you saying you think it might have been... supernatural?" She was skeptical, but willing to hear him out.

I don't know. All I know is we don't have answers for everything yet.

Sam seemed accepting that they might never know, but the uncertainty still gnawed at her. She tried to focus on something else, knowing there was nothing she could do to figure it out right now, and once their appetites began to slow down, Sadie took the chance to broach a topic she had been meaning to talk to Sam about for a while.

"I've been thinking more about Rose and Briar," she said. "They need something to do, especially Briar, and I told you about how much Sheriff Islington could use a good tracking dog…"

Sam put down his chopsticks again to sign, *I don't want to adopt them out to someone else.*

"No, of course not," she said quickly. "You would be their handler. The sheriff even said he'd be able to pay a little, so it wouldn't be volunteer work... not completely, anyway."

Sam shook his head. *I can't do it.*

Sadie frowned, confused. "Why not?"

I can't talk to someone through a radio, Sadie, he signed. *I can't call out or talk to a lost or injured person. I can't call to tell the police my location or request an ambulance. If we're tracking someone dangerous, I won't be able to communicate with law enforcement. I want to do it. But I can't.*

He picked his chopsticks back up, signaling the end of the conversation, and Sadie felt her cheeks pinken. It was easy to forget that he had a disability, especially now that she knew enough sign language to carry on a fluent conversation with him. But the truth was, his inability to speak would always limit him in some ways.

"Sorry," she muttered, feeling awkward. "I didn't think of that."

He gave a stiff shrug, and they finished the rest of their meal in silence.

CHAPTER TEN

Hoping to mend the sudden discomfort between them, Sadie suggested they stop at Sunshine Desserts after lunch. Sam agreed to go, but she thought he still seemed a little off.

Being the middle of the day on a Sunday, the little cookie shop was busy. While they waited, they looked through the display cases, trying to decide what to get. The cookie shop had a number of regular offerings – the classics and favorites that were always available – but it also regularly had new recipes. Bailey was a skilled baker and seemed to have an endless well of creativity.

Sadie spotted some sugar cookies that stood out because of their ornate icing, which was painstakingly colored and shaped to resemble the local wildflowers that grew everywhere at this time of year. She immediately decided she had to get a couple; they were gorgeous, and she knew Penny would love them.

The door opened behind them, and Sadie glanced over her shoulder to see Hunter come in. He was carrying a few papers, receipts, maybe, or order form, and was looking them over as he walked, so he didn't notice them as he went past and joined Bailey behind the counter. While she rang up the person ahead of them, he pointed something out on one of the papers and murmured to her, only to break the conversation off when he spotted the two of them.

"Oh, hey," he said as the customer in front of them accepted their receipt and walked away. "I didn't see you guys when I came in. I heard someone died at the motel yesterday."

Bailey shushed him, looked around at the other customers, then urged Sadie and Sam further down the counter to where they would have at least a pretense of privacy.

"Hush, Hunter," she said. "They probably don't want that spread around."

"How did the two of you hear about it?" Sadie asked.

"Do you know Loretta Browning?" Bailey asked.

Sadie nodded, her eyes narrowing. "We're familiar with her."

"She came in this morning, all sorts of gleeful." The younger woman rolled her eyes. "I swear, that woman has a vicious streak a mile wide. She told us about it while she was picking out cookies for the wave of guests she hoped would be driven away from your motel and flood her bed and breakfast. How *she* knew, I have no idea, but it wouldn't surprise me if that woman had a network of spies around town."

Sadie raised an eyebrow. "You're talking like she's some sort of mastermind."

Bailey gave her a rueful smile. "I'm exaggerating... mostly. She used to be a pretty prominent figure in town. Ten years ago, her son died in a car accident while he was visiting with his wife, and after that, she withdrew almost entirely. She went from heading a good chunk of the local community and volunteer groups, to locking herself inside of that big old house of hers and rarely coming out. I wasn't even sure if she was still alive, to be honest. I haven't seen her for over six months, but something seems to have given her a new lease on life."

Sadie suspected she knew what that was; their motel. Or rather, the competition they offered.

For now, Loretta seemed harmless enough, so

maybe giving her a fresh lease on life was a good thing. Changing the subject, Sadie lowered her voice.

"What exactly did you tell the vloggers yesterday, by the way? I'm a little worried about what I'm going to see when they release the footage."

"I told the truth," he said, his lips twitching. "Well, I might have hyped up some of the supernatural stuff a little bit. It'll be great for business, though. People love haunted houses and hotels."

Sadie scowled at him. "You told them the place was haunted?"

"They're the ones who asked me whether there had been any supernatural occurrences there," he said defensively. "I didn't lie, just… stretched the truth a little."

"Hunter, I asked you to stick to the facts," Sadie said.

Bailey crossed her arms and glared at her employee. "Great job, Hunter. What if Sadie and Penny decide to sue us for defamation?"

"They aren't going to do that," Hunter said, though he looked worried. "Look, I'll fix it. I'm giving them a tour of town tomorrow, and I'll tell them I was just kidding around."

"You'd better," Bailey muttered. She glanced at Sadie. "Sorry about that."

"As long as he fixes it," Sadie said. She was still unhappy about it, but it was too late to change whatever he had told them.

"He will," Bailey replied, the edge in her voice leaving no doubt that she would be furious if he didn't.

Hunter gave them a wounded look, then glanced at the clock. "Shoot, I've got to hurry. I have to get that delivery ready for the nursing home. See ya."

He gave them a salute and hurried into the back of the cookie shop. Bailey rolled her eyes.

"I'll make sure he makes things right," she promised. "I suspect he was trying to impress Tanisha with his ghost stories. He's barely stopped talking about her all weekend."

"At least that means he's over Penny," Sadie said.

Sam gave a huff of laughter, then she smiled at him, glad things were getting back to normal.

"We should probably stop holding my other customers up," Bailey asked, pushing away from the counter. "How many cookies can I get you today?"

CHAPTER ELEVEN

The rest of Sadie's Sunday was subdued. She had some brief fun with Penny, admiring and then eating the gorgeous sugar cookies, but that light-heartedness faded quickly, overcome with the sadness and uncertainty from Allen's death. He might have been annoying, trying to push a service on them that they had repeatedly told him they didn't want, but that didn't mean she wanted him *dead*. With the uncertainty came guilt. What if his death had been preventable, the consequence of exposure to some sort of gas she and Penny hadn't known to test for?

Once again, she did what she always did when she was upset and buried herself in work with the dogs. By the time she went to bed, all of the dogs had gotten long walks, playtime, and had freshly washed bedding. She said goodnight to Penny, neither of them mentioning the sensitive topic of the fog Sadie had seen. They seemed to be at an impasse for now, and she didn't want to go to bed on a sour note.

As the dogs settled down in her room, Sadie sat up with her back cushioned against the pillows. She was tired, but her mind was too full of thoughts for her to sleep, so she grabbed a book, a science fiction thriller about creatures that lived underground, lent to her by Sam, from her bedside table and began to read.

When she woke up, the windows were still dark, but the bedside lamp was on, and her book was sprawled face down on the bed next to her. She was disoriented and felt that something was missing, but it wasn't until she looked around the room and spotted both dogs standing in front of the window, their heads tilted to the side, that she realized what must have woken her: Jasper's absence, or perhaps whatever the two dogs had heard outside.

"What did you hear?" she murmured.

Both dogs were standing stock still. Jasper's ear twitched when she spoke, but he didn't look away from the window. She felt a chill go down her spine but reminded herself that she was on the second story. Whatever had got their attention couldn't get in and it was probably just an owl or fox, anyway.

She reached over to turn off the lamp on the bedside table, knowing she wouldn't be able to see a thing outside with her room illuminated, then eased out of bed and tiptoed over to the window, standing next to the dogs as she pulled the curtains back and looked out.

Movement. Something pale was walking on the dark road, outside of the circle of light that illuminated the parking lot. For a heart-stopping second, her sleep-addled brain thought it was one of those creatures in the book she was reading, but then common sense took over. It had to be a person, except the shape was amorphous and fog swirled out from under the pale robes that it was wearing.

As she watched, a horrible moan came from the thing, loud enough that she could hear it through the glass. Angus put his front feet up on the windowsill and began to growl low in his throat. Jasper whined and leaned against her leg.

Sadie's heart pounded like it was trying to hammer its way out of her chest. Jittery with fear, she scurried back to her nightstand, unplugged her phone, and opened her camera app, intending to take a video of the thing. But by the time she returned to the window, it was gone.

Gone, or out of sight. She yanked the curtains

shut, then went to sit on her bed as she pulled up the security footage. To her dismay, there weren't any new notifications, which meant the thing hadn't been caught on camera. She brought up the live footage from the camera over the lobby door, but the angle was all wrong: it only caught a fraction of the parking lot and nothing on the road. She brought up the footage from the camera that looked out along the row of rooms. This had a wider view of the area in front of the motel, at least… it usually did. Right now, the image was completely black, as if something was blocking the lens.

Swallowing with a mouth that had gone dry, Sadie dialed Penny's number. It rang through to voicemail twice, but on the third ring her friend picked up, her voice groggy.

"What?"

"Something's wrong," Sadie said. "Someone's outside, and the footage from the second camera is blocked."

"Huh?" She heard rustling and assumed Penny was sitting up in bed.

Sadie repeated herself, then added, "We need to figure out what's going on. I'm going to call Sam."

"I guess I'll get up too," Penny said. She still sounded more sleepy than worried.

"Don't go outside until I'm down there," she warned.

She felt bad for waking Sam up, but knew he would want her to, and that it would be dangerous and, frankly, stupid for her and Penny to investigate the pale figure she had seen without his help. She called him, and when he answered, she hung up and texted him a brief summary of what was going on. A moment later, he texted back, *I'll be over in two minutes.*

She got her shoes on, grabbed her pepper spray, flashlight, and phone, and stared out the window until she saw his truck turn into the parking lot. Good, he hadn't walked over in the dark. Leaving the dogs upstairs, she hurried down to the lobby and unlocked the door just as he was getting out of his truck. Briar, his big male coonhound, was with him, and Sam had a fire axe in the other hand. She waved, then turned at the sound of a door opening. Penny was joining them.

"Let's check the camera first," Sadie said. With their heads on swivels, they made their way over to the camera at the very end of the row of rooms. Sadie aimed her flashlight up at it and saw what looked like a stiff piece of black paper over the lens.

"What the heck?" Penny said, squinting. She sounded like she was realizing something was actually wrong. "Someone blocked the camera on purpose."

Sam handed Sadie Briar's leash, then went back to his truck to get a step ladder out of the back. Setting it up, he climbed up and pulled the piece of paper off of the camera lens, pausing to polish it with the hem of his shirt before he came back down and showed the paper to Penny and Sadie. It had some sort of sticky putty on the side that had been attached to the lens.

"We should check the footage," Penny said. "It might have caught whoever did this."

Sadie shook her head. "I doubt it. If they wanted to block the camera, they would have made sure to stay out of sight while they did so. They probably used a stick or something to get this paper up there. We can still check, but I'd be surprised if we found anything."

Sam temporarily put his axe down to sign, *Let's look around. Maybe they're still here.*

Sadie nodded, and the three of them slowly made their way around the motel, shining their lights into every nook and cranny and along the line of the woods, but whatever she had seen wasn't hanging around anymore.

They retreated to the lobby and locked the door

behind them. Sadie briefly went into the kennel room to check on the boarding dogs, then returned to the others, patting Briar as she came back into the lobby. Penny already had her laptop open, and the live security footage pulled up so they could keep an eye on the cameras.

"What exactly did you see, Sadie?" Penny asked. "Did you recognize any of the person's features?"

"No," Sadie said. She hesitated, knowing what it was going to sound like, but she forged ahead anyway. "The person I saw was wearing something like a white robe that covered them from head to toe, and they were surrounded by a swirl of fog."

Penny gave her a flat, disbelieving look. "You saw a ghost?"

"It wasn't a ghost," Sadie said. "What sort of ghost would stick a piece of paper to a camera before making an appearance?"

Her friend pressed her lips together. "Well, I agree that someone had to have been out there — otherwise, why block the footage? But you must have been half asleep when you saw them."

"I know what I saw," Sadie snapped back, crossing her arms. "I know how it sounds, Penny, but I'm not crazy and I'm not imagining things."

"You're asking me to believe in ghosts," Penny

said, throwing her arms wide. "And okay, maybe it's easy to believe in them when it's night and I'm creeped out, but ghosts aren't real. Not really. The logical explanation is that you saw a living person, but you were still half asleep when you saw them."

Sadie opened her mouth to retort, but Sam put a hand on her shoulder and squeezed. When she turned toward him, he signed, *Do you want me to stay tonight?* She nodded, letting her breath out with a whoosh.

"Do you want to come upstairs too?" she asked Penny. "I hate the thought of you being down here alone."

Her friend shook her head. She glanced at Sadie, then looked away. "No, I should stay down here in case the guests need something. We'll talk about this more in the morning, all right? I'm sure things will feel better in the daylight."

Sadie and Sam stood outside the lobby to make sure Penny got safely back into her room. Only after Sadie heard the deadbolt turn did she retreat inside the lobby and lock the door behind them. Upstairs, the dogs happily greeted Sam. Thankfully, Briar had slowly come to tolerate Jasper and gave the overly friendly foxhound a cursory sniff before laying down on the rug in the middle of the living room with a grumble. Sadie shooed the other two dogs back into her room before fetching fresh linens to make the couch up for Sam. They were both too restless to sleep, so she sat up with him for a while, the lights on dim so they could talk.

"I'm sorry about yesterday," she said. "I wasn't thinking."

He shook his head and signed, *It's not your fault, and I wasn't mad at you. I was...* He hesitated, his hands hanging in the hair. *Ashamed. I want to be able to do all the things I would be able to do if I was normal, especially the things you want to do. And I hate knowing I can't.*

She leaned forward and hugged him. "It's nothing to be ashamed of," she said, "and it's no big deal, really. How would you feel if we found a different handler for Briar and Rose? They would still be your dogs, but someone else could take them out when the sheriff needs help tracking someone through the woods. That way you can still be involved in their training, they'll have jobs to keep them occupied, and the sheriff will have his tracking dogs without spending an arm and a leg to get one."

He gave a huff of laughter. *There isn't always going to be a solution for everything,* he signed, *but I'm glad there is this time.*

CHAPTER TWELVE

There were no more apparitions or strange sounds that night. Sadie and Sam had enough time to drink their coffee together before he had to leave to feed Briar and Rose and get started with his day, and she had to go down to the kennel to get started with hers. Things between her and Penny felt fragile, and even when her friend apologized later that morning, it didn't help much.

"I shouldn't have said all of that last night," she said. "We were all tired and tensions were high. I know you wouldn't make things up, Sadie."

"But you still don't believe me," Sadie said. Her friend frowned.

"I know you're not lying. I just…"

"You think I'm hallucinating."

Her friend wouldn't meet her eyes, and they spent the next few hours going about their day in tense silence. A little before ten, Hunter arrived in the Sunshine Desserts delivery van, and Sadie saw Tanisha climb into the passenger seat with Emily's camera in hand. She frowned, wondering where Emily was, but was distracted by Maria coming in, triumphantly clutching an envelope full of cash. She looked at Sadie briefly, her expression guilty, then turned to Penny.

"Here you go," she said, "just as I promised. I also included enough to stay for the rest of the week, if that's okay."

"Great, we'll get you booked in," Penny said.

She looked relieved that Maria had actually paid them. Sadie would have been too, but she found she didn't care anymore. Maria was lying, and until she came clean, she didn't want anything to do with the other woman.

Sadie was out front pulling weeds from the mulch-covered flower beds in front of the motel when Hunter and Tanisha returned. They were both smiling as they got out of the van, and Tanisha's cheeks darkened with a blush as she placed a quick kiss on Hunter's cheek.

"Thanks for the tour," she said. "I loved learning so much about the town and the surrounding area. Do you want to come in and see some of the footage I got today?"

"I'd love to," Hunter said. "Just give me a second, I have to shut the van off."

Sadie stood up, putting her gloved hands on her hips as she watched Tanisha walk back to her motel room. As the other woman unlocked the door to Room Ten, Sadie's gaze fixed on Hunter instead. He caught her look and walked over, his expression sheepish.

"Don't worry, I told her I was just kidding about all the ghost stuff," he said. "Mostly. I mean, there are some creepy things, like how so many people died in Room—"

He broke off when a piercing scream came from the far end of the row of motel rooms. Tanisha raced out of Room Ten, and, catching sight of them, ran in their direction. They met her halfway. As she passed the door to Room Nine, it opened and Emily peered out at the commotion.

"What happened?" Sadie asked as Tanisha clung to her arm and looked back over her shoulder, frightened.

"My room," she said. "Look at it."

Sadie strode forward as Tanisha released her grip on her arm. She and Hunter followed, and Emily joined them.

"What's going on?" she murmured.

"I have no idea," Sadie told her. They passed Room Nine and came Room Ten. Sadie looked inside and felt her face go pale. There was something red dripping down the walls, and Tanisha's clothing was strewn all over the room like a hurricane had come through. Some of the shirts were ripped and torn to tatters.

"I didn't—" Tanisha's voice was shaking. "Everything was neatly packed away when I left, and the blood wasn't—" She broke off and fell into Hunter's arms, sobbing.

"No way, it really *is* haunted," he breathed.

"The motel is not haunted," Sadie snapped.

She glanced up and saw that another piece of paper had been stuck over the security camera, then stepped into the room and looked around. There was no sign of the fog, which was a relief. It didn't appear that the walls or furniture had been damaged. She frowned and reached out to touch the blood before rubbing it between her fingers. It was sticky and translucent, and most importantly, it didn't smell like blood. In fact, it both smelled and felt familiar. The last time she had seen something like this was on Halloween.

Gingerly, she lifted her finger to her mouth and tasted it.

"Oh, my goodness, I'm going to be sick," Tanisha moaned.

"It's fake blood," Sadie said, "just… a lot of it." She looked around the room, wondering just how hard it would be to clean off the walls.

"What's happening?" She turned to see Maria join the group that was standing outside the room. The older woman looked confused but then gasped when she saw the fake blood on the walls.

"That's what I'm trying to figure out," Sadie said. She walked back out of the room, then glanced at Emily.

"Do you mind if we look into your room, too? I want to see if any of the other rooms have been vandalized."

Wide-eyed, Emily shook her head and handed over her key. Sadie unlocked the door and stepped inside. This room was untouched. Sadie looked around, and her eyes fixed on Emily's laptop, which was open on the desk, an image from a video paused on the screen.

It was the ghost she had seen last night. Like she

was in a trance, Sadie walked closer and tapped the spacebar to play the video. The footage seemed to have been taken inside of Emily's room, with the camera looking out over the road as the ghost glided through the darkness, fog swirling around it.

"Oh, that's cool," Hunter said, peering over her shoulder. "What is that smoky stuff? Dry ice?"

Reality crashed over her. First was the validation that came from Hunter's words: she wasn't going crazy. The figure had been real, and so was the fog — and along with that relief came an explanation that made sense. Dry ice. She had seen it used before in haunted houses and at parties. She didn't know why she hadn't made the connection sooner.

"That's for a creative project–" Emily started.

She moved to shut the computer, but Sadie held it open. She exited the window that the footage was playing in and saw a list of different video files in the open file explorer. She clicked one at random. It was footage from a dark forest… the motel's forest. She recognized the old, falling-down shed by the overgrown flower garden. Eerie mist was curling out of the windows, undoubtedly the effects of more dry ice.

Shaking, not with fear but with anger, she took a step back, letting Emily shut the laptop, and looked around the room. Her gaze fixed on the vent in the wall. She knew there was one directly opposite it in Room Eight, and the small fan on the floor was still there… pointed right at it.

CHAPTER THIRTEEN

Livid, Sadie turned to face the others, her mind racing. The answer seemed obvious, but she had to be sure, because there was more than one person with a motive to play this kind of hoax. Loretta, though she was an old woman, was surprisingly spry for her age, and she had a reason to want to drive guests away from the motel. Faking a haunting seemed like something that might be right up her alley. And then there was Hunter—had all of this been a poorly thought-out prank to validate his ghost stories? He looked just as confused and surprised as she felt, and while she wouldn't put it past him to do something like make a fake paranormal video, she didn't think he would continue after someone died.

She looked at Maria next.

"Why did you lie?" she asked. "About the fog." Maria shook her head, but Sadie retorted, "Don't deny it. You made me feel like I was crazy, and you lied to the police. Why?"

Maria bowed her head. "My kids," she explained. "I'm going through a divorce, and my husband has money and influence. He's trying to take everything, including full custody of the kids. I'm afraid he'll try to get his lawyer to use every little thing he can find against me, and if I started talking about weird mist and ghosts, that might be enough for the judge to decide I should get minimal custody of them. I'm sorry, but I would do anything to keep my kids."

Sadie clenched her jaw, thinking. She believed Maria, but the woman had already proven to be a liar, so she wasn't sure if she should go with her gut on this one. But what reason would Maria have to fake a haunting? It didn't make sense. Besides, she would have had to be working with Tanisha and Emily, and Sadie hadn't seen any sign that she knew them.

She looked at Tanisha next, feeling betrayed. She had let the two of them come to the motel and invade everyone's privacy, and they had turned around and thrown it all back in her face.

"You've been doing this, haven't you? You thought you could come here and use our motel to boost your viewership. Do you have any idea what you've done? Someone's dead because of you, and you lied to us—"

"She didn't know about any of this," Emily interrupted. She stepped forward and took a shaky breath. "I did it. All right? I did all of it. I never meant to kill anyone, but it's my fault."

Tanisha whirled to stare at the younger woman, her eyes going wide. "Emily, what are you talking about?"

Emily couldn't meet her gaze, so she spoke to Sadie instead. "I've been a huge fan of Tanisha's for a long time, and when she hired me to be her videographer, I felt like the luckiest person in the world. Not only was it my dream job, but it was with my favorite vlogger. I was worried about her viewership not rising quickly enough, and I thought that we could make things a little more interesting if we added some scripted surprises. But she always wanted her videos to be genuine, and vetoed my ideas for a script... so I started doing little things: secretly paying people to approach us, editing some of the footage so it looks like things happened in a different order than they really did... and then, when I read about the history of this place, I thought faking a haunting would be the perfect thing to do next."

Tanisha looked at her in betrayal. "You've been doing all of that in secret? It's my channel, Emily! I didn't want any of this to happen!"

"I know," Emily blinked, tears brimming in her eyes. "I never meant to hurt anyone. I told Tanisha I heard creepy sounds coming from that room overnight, then later that day, I put the dry ice just inside the register and used the fan to blow the mist into Room Eight. I knew Maria was cleaning in there. I thought she would see and get spooked. It was supposed to be a harmless prank, but then it took her a long time to come back, and I didn't realize that man went in the room. Dry ice gives off carbon dioxide when it evaporates, and if he shut the door behind him, it must have displaced enough of the air to make him suffocate. If he drifted off, he might not have even noticed what was happening."

"Carbon dioxide," Sadie murmured. "The carbon monoxide detectors wouldn't have detected it. That ghost I saw last night was you, too?"

"And my room?" Tanisha asked.

Emily nodded, morose. "Yeah, the ghost was me, dressed in a sheet with some dry ice in a packet tied to my boots. I covered the security camera earlier in the day, set my camera up on the windowsill, and went outside to walk back and forth on the road.

When I saw the light go off upstairs, I realized someone might be watching me, so I put on a show, then hid." Now she did glance at Tanisha. "I'm sorry about your room. I only tore up the shirts I knew you hated. I thought it would look more real if you were genuinely freaked out."

"You killed someone, Emily," Tanisha said, looking at her in horror. "I don't approve of the rest of it, but I can understand why you did it—we wouldn't be the first people in this industry to fake a paranormal encounter—but why in the world would you keep going after someone died?"

"It was a fluke," Emily said. "I didn't mean to. It was just an accident."

"It was a fatal one," Sadie said grimly. "And I hope you're ready to face the consequences of it."

EPILOGUE

"I'm sorry, sir, but your information is wrong. We don't have any ghosts here."

The man who stood across from her looked disappointed. "Are you sure? Because I saw this video online–"

"That was a hoax," Sadie repeated for what felt like the hundredth time. In reality, he was only the third ghost hunter who had visited the motel since Tanisha released her video. Despite the disclaimer at the end that it had all been a hoax by her ex-videographer, a lot of people seemed to have either missed that part or didn't believe it.

"Are you sure?" he repeated. He looked so heartbroken that she relented.

"You're welcome to stay for a few nights and see for yourself, but we require an extra fee for anyone who's going to be filming on the premises."

A new policy, mainly because she and Penny had decided that having people filming here was more trouble than it was worth… but if someone wanted to pay, they were welcome to.

The man eagerly dug into his pocket for his wallet. At least the video was bringing them some more business, even if it hadn't happened quite how Sadie had hoped. She gave the man the key to his room, then sat down on the spinning chair behind the front desk and leaned back with a sigh.

Things were back to normal now, for the most part. Maria had found a cheap room to rent in town, though Penny had agreed to hire her to come back and clean twice a week. Sadie wasn't thrilled, but she wasn't about to veto it either. Maria *did* do a great job of deep cleaning the rooms, and even though she still disliked the woman for lying, she understood why she had done it. Cody, who had missed most of the excitement from the weekend Tanisha and Emily stayed, was just glad that they had another part-time worker to take some of the menial labor off of his shoulders.

With summer now upon them and people beginning to take more vacations and road trips, business was ramping up again. There was a lot they wanted to accomplish this year, and with the extra money they were getting from the additional traffic through the motel, it wouldn't be long before they could afford their first major upgrades.

Printed in Dunstable, United Kingdom